D1093636

Ravi's Diwali
Surprise

by Anisha Kacker

Illustrated by
Kusum Ohri

MULTICULTURAL CELEBRATIONS II

MODERN CURRICULUM PRESS

Multicultural Celebrations was created under the auspices of
The Children's Museum, Boston.
Leslie Swartz, Director of Teacher Services,
directed this project.

Design: Gary Fujiwara
Photographs: 6, Air-India Library,
17, Anisha Kacker.

MODERN CURRICULUM PRESS, INC.
13900 Prospect Road
Cleveland, Ohio 44136

ISBN 0-8136-2333-2 (soft cover)   0-8136-2334-0 (hard cover)

1 2 3 4 5 6 7 8 9 10   98 97 96 95 94

Simon & Schuster   A Paramount Communications Company

Ravi was up by 6 o'clock this chilly October morning.
He had something on his mind. It was the day of *Diwali*,
the Indian festival of lights.

"I know I promised to help get ready for the celebration,"
he thought to himself, "but it's just not the same this
year."

Ravi tiptoed downstairs. Mummy was already in the kitchen. She had started to prepare the *gulab jamuns*. Ravi loved these cottage cheese balls filled with raisins and almonds and dipped in syrup.

"Well, good morning. You're up early," his mother greeted him.

"When will the Pandit's and Ayushi be here?" he asked.

"Not this early!" his mother laughed. "They're driving from New Jersey this afternoon. They'll be here in time for the evening prayer service. And don't forget about Shankar."

"Well, Shankar sure has forgotten about me," said Ravi frowning. His older brother had left for college early in September. Here it was October and Ravi had not heard a thing from him. He hadn't written — he hadn't called.

"Forgotten you? You can't believe that! You're unforgettable," said Mummy laughing. "But he may be late. Right now we have food to fix, and the shrine to put up. And your father will need help with the lights."

The lights made *Diwali* one of Ravi's favorite holidays. *Diwali* celebrates the ancient story of the return of good Prince Ram to his people. They gave him a welcome by lighting hundreds and hundreds of *diyas,* clay oil lamps.

5

"This is one of our happiest times of the year. Can you give me just one smile?" his mother asked.

Shaking his head, Ravi took his place at the chopping board. He cut vegetables and rolled dough for *samosas*. Mummy was making *mithai*, creamy sweets. These snacks would be shared later with their visitors. The morning went quickly.

"Ravi, let's decorate the shrine," called his dad from the living room. "We have to be ready for tonight's *puja*."

Together they brought out the small statues of *Lakshmi,* the goddess of good fortune and *Ganesh,* the god of luck.

"*Ganesh* always looks content, " Ravi said.

"Yes, but that's not how you have looked lately," his father said. "Do you remember the stories about *Ganesh?* How he overcame all problems. He had faith — and luck came to him. Ravi, you must have faith too."

Together they hung pictures of other Hindu gods and goddesses around the shrine. Then they put out the flowers, the *diyas,* and candles.

"Now for the outside lights," Mr Tandon said.

9

"No, not yet..." Ravi said.

"But Ravi, we want the house to be all lit up for the celebration."

"Can't we wait just a little while?" Ravi thought maybe just a little faith wouldn't hurt.

"Of course," his father answered, finally understanding. Every *Diwali* before this, Ravi and Shankar had put up the lights together.

After lunch, everyone put on their new clothes, as they do for *Diwali*. Ravi put on his new *kurta* over long pants. His mother dressed in a silk *sari*. She also put a *bindi*, the traditional red dot, on her forehead, as most women in India do.

10

Late in the afternoon, a car pulled up. Ravi ran to see who it was. "The Pandit's are here," he called to his mother.

"You sound a little disappointed."

"Oh, no... it's just that I think we can't wait any longer to put up the lights," Ravi said. "Ayushi can help me."

"*Namaste, namaste. Diwali mubarak,*" greeted Ravi, wishing the guests a happy *Diwali*.

Shankar or no Shankar, soon they would begin the celebration.

Ravi and Ayushi started to hang strings of lights
along the porch railing. Then Ravi stood on a chair
to reach top of the windows. The chair wobbled a little.

"Ayushi, hold the chair steady while I hook these lights," he
called without looking down. The chair wobbled again.
"Ayushi…"

"Ayushi went inside. Will I do as a helper?" a familiar
voice asked.

"Shankar! You're home!" Ravi cried, almost falling.

Shankar smiled. "What's the story? I went away for
two months and you've already forgotten that we do
the *Diwali* lights together?"

"I hadn't forgotten, but I thought you had." Ravi said.

14

"No, Ravi. School has kept me very busy. But you must believe I would never miss spending *Diwali* with my best pal!" Then he grabbed Ravi around the waist, pretending to wrestle as they always did.

Hearing the laughter from the front porch, everyone rushed out to greet Shankar. "Ravi, calm down. You'll ruin your *kurta!*" mummy warned.

Together Ravi and Shankar hung the rest of the lights. Everyone gathered in the living room.

They all sang the *aarti* and Mrs. Pandit rang a small
bell. Father held the *thali* with a *diya* on it. With this
tray he formed a circle of light in front of the shrine.
Rice, flowers, and *mithai* offered to the gods. Would
they bring good fortune to the family?

Ravi and Shankar sat together. Ravi felt he had the luck
of *Ganesh* and the good fortune of *Lakshmi...* all the
good things Diwali promised. Shankar had returned to
hundreds and hundreds of lights.

20

Glossary

aarti (AHR-tee) a Hindu prayer song

bindi (BIHN-dee) a red dot worn on the forehead of Indian women

diya (DEE-yuh) a clay oil lamp

gulab jamuns (GOO-lahb jahmunz) fried cheese balls filled with raisins and almonds

kurta (KUHR-ta) a long-tailed shirt worn over slacks

mithai (mi-TEYE) creamy sweets

puja (POO-juh) an evening prayer service

samosas (sa-MO-suhz) rolled dough filled with potatoes or other vegetables

sari (SAH-ree) a wrap-around gown worn by women in India

About the Author

Anisha Kacker was born and raised in New Delhi, India where she completed her Master's Degree in History from the University of Delhi. She came to the United States in 1990. Anisha Kacker is now the librarian at the Resource Center, The Children's Museum, Boston, after having finished a Master's Degree in Library Science from Simmons College, Boston.

About the Illustrator

Kusum Ohri is a painter, illustrator, and teacher. She was born in Jamshedpur, India and came to the United States in 1962 with her family. Here she earned a masters and doctorate degree from the University of Maryland. She currently teaches art in Rockville, Maryland, and exhibits her work at local galleries.

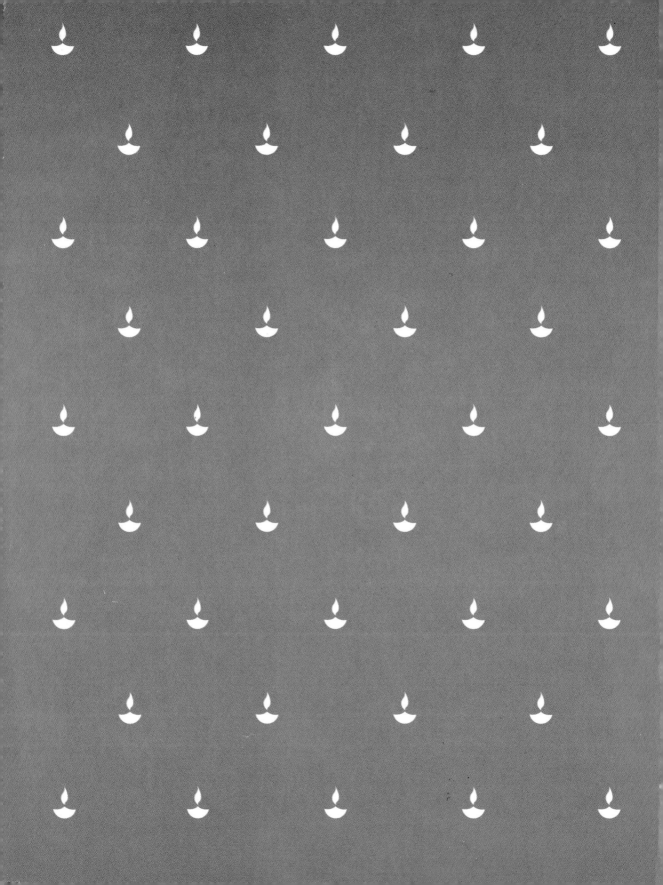